WITHDRAWN

Paid for by donations

from the

Mount Laurel Community

Ripley's Believe It or Not!

Developed and produced by Ripley Publishing Ltd

This edition published and distributed by:
Mason Crest Publishers Inc.
370 Reed Road, Broomall, Pennsylvania 19008
(866) MCP-BOOK (toll free)
www.masoncrest.com

Copyright © 2011 by Mason Crest Publishers. All rights reserved. No part of this publication may be reproduced or transmitted in any form or by any means, electronic or mechanical, including photocopying, recording, taping, or any information storage and retrieval system, without permission from the publisher.

Ripley's Believe it or Not!
Strange World
ISBN 978-1-4222-2027-6 (hardcover)
ISBN 978-1-4222-2061-0 (paperback)

Library of Congress Cataloging-in-Publication data is available

Ripley's Believe it or Not!—Complete 16 Title Series
ISBN 978-1-4222-2014-6

1st printing
10 9 8 7 6 5 4 3 2 1

Library of Congress Cataloging-in-Publication Data is available.
Printed in USA

PUBLISHER'S NOTE
While every effort has been made to verify the accuracy of the entries in this book, the Publisher's cannot be held responsible for any errors contained in the work. They would be glad to receive any information from readers.

WARNING
Some of the stunts and activities in this book are undertaken by experts and should not be attempted by anyone without adequate training and supervision.

Expect... The Unexpected

Mason Crest Publishers

STRANGE WORLD

On another planet. If you already thought the world was a bit mad, you'll think it's bonkers when you get a load of this book! Read about the elephant with two trunks, the boa constrictor that appeared in a toilet, and the spooky glow in the dark gravestone.

Eiliv Ruud walks across crevasses and canyons on a thin wire thousands of feet above the ground...

Crazy Horse

The detailed face of Crazy Horse stands 87 ft 6 in (26.7 m) high and took 50 years to complete—the lips alone took two years and the nose is 27 ft (8.2 m) long!

More than 8 million tons of rock has been blasted from a South Dakota mountain to create a sculpture depicting Native American chief Crazy Horse, who led the Oglala Sioux at the battle of the Little Bighorn in 1876.

With arm outstretched toward his ancestral homeland, astride a stallion over two football fields long, Crazy Horse will be 641 ft (195 m) long and 563 ft (172 m) high. By comparison, the heads of Mount Rushmore are a mere 60 ft (18 m) high.

At the invitation of local Indian leaders, Boston-born sculptor Korczak Ziolkowski began work on Thunderhead Mountain back in 1948. The crew uses precision explosive engineering to remove and shape the mountain rock, with explosives loaded into holes drilled to a depth of 35 ft (11 m). The final surface is smoothed by a jet torch, which operates at 3,300°F (1,815°C).

With the face complete, work is now progressing on the horse's head, which will stand 219 ft (66.7 m) high—the equivalent of a staggering 22 stories. To achieve this, another 4 million tons of granite must be removed.

The final memorial will also feature a poem written by Ziolkowski, which will be carved into the hard mountain rock in letters 3 ft (1 m) tall.

STRANGE WORLD

Sharpshooters
Since 1971, the World Peashooting Championship has been held in the village of Witcham, England. Some competitors take the event so seriously that they fit their shooters with laser or telescopic sights for a better aim.

In SADIEVILLE, Kentucky, property owners are banned by law from mowing their lawns, but fishing in the nude is legal.

Mud Slinging
In South Korea each summer, families, friends, and complete strangers indulge in hours of mud slinging—and enjoy every minute of it. They are taking part in the annual Poryong Mud Festival, a mad, muddy mess that features mud baths, mud sculpture, mud body-painting, and even a mud beauty contest. Hundreds of willing competitors seize the opportunity to get grubby, encouraged by the beneficial minerals in the local mud, which are believed to reduce wrinkles and wash away excess oils from the skin.

Quick Service
At Lambert's Café, Sikeston, Missouri, they don't bring the rolls in a basket—they throw them at you! One day in 1976, the restaurant was so busy that proprietor Norman Lambert was unable to get through the crowd to serve the rolls. A customer shouted, "Throw it!" and Lambert did—and the tradition began.

▶ How Many Hooves?
This six-legged calf was born on a farm in Poland in February 2005. It belongs to farmer Jaroslaw Garbal, who has named the animal "Star."

Message in a Bottle
William T. Mullen's wife warned him that if he didn't stop drinking she would humiliate him after his death. He paid no attention and died in 1863, whereupon she carried out her threat by giving him a gravestone—at Clayton, Alabama—in the shape of a whiskey bottle.

Barking Beach
Believe it or not, Barking Sands Beach, on the Hawaiian island of Kauai, has sand that barks like a dog! The dry sand grains emit this strange sound when you walk on them in bare feet.

Chocolate Moose
Lenny the Moose is made from 1,700 lb (771 kg) of the finest milk chocolate! A life-sized chocolate moose, Lenny resides at Len Libby Handmade Candies in Scarborough, Maine. He was born in 1997 at the request of the store's co-owner Maureen Hemond, and created on-site in four weeks by local sculptor Zdeno Mayercak. The moose is 8 ft (2.4 m) tall and over 9 ft (2.7 m) from nose to tail. He began as a metal armature onto which 10-lb (4.5-kg) chocolate blocks were placed. Melted chocolate was then used as the mortar to hold the blocks together.

STRANGE WORLD

▶ **Two-trunked!**
Ripley's took possession of this preserved head in August 2005—the elephant itself had been shot in Zimbabwe on November 9, 2004. It is estimated that the animal was about five years old. The head was preserved, and DNA analysis has determined that the two trunks contain identical DNA patterns and that they were indeed from the same animal.

Ripley's Believe It or Not!®

Dearly Departed

★ Scotsman Alexander, Duke of Hamilton, spent more than £11,500 ($20,000) on a genuine ancient Egyptian coffin. But, when he died in 1852, he was found to be too long for it and so his legs had to be cut off before he could fit inside.

★ In 1876, an American gang of grave robbers tried unsuccessfully to steal Abraham Lincoln's body and hold it for ransom in return for the release of a convicted forger, Ben Boyd.

★ When the body of King George IV of England became badly swollen in his coffin, court attendants feared that it would explode through the lining. So, they hurriedly drilled a hole in the casket to let out some of the rotten air.

Dead Weird!

Wacky gravestones are all the rage in Japan. In a land where household altars and ornate headstones are the norm, specialist shops sell extraordinary-looking sculptures for remembering the dead. A gravestone shop in Fuji stocks such offbeat stone sculptures as Godzilla, a hippopotamus, and a baby dinosaur breaking through an egg. At a gravestone design competition in Japan in 2005, every taste was catered for, as shown above, left, and below.

▲ Glow in the Dark

An Austrian company is selling solar-powered glow-in-the-dark gravestones. The grave appears normal during daylight hours, but once it gets dark the grave begins to glow. A family grave, large enough to hold 12 bodies, has already been constructed. The standard single version comes with a glowing gravestone, a solar roof, and a digital text display that allows relatives to program in names, the date of death, and personal blessings.

STRANGE WORLD

Miracle Putt
There should be no cursing on a miniature golf course at Lexington, Kentucky—because the 54-hole course has a biblical theme throughout. The first 18 holes are based on events in the Old Testament, the second 18 are related to the New Testament, and the final 18 are the toughest—the miracles. Where else can you play through Jesus's tomb and Jonah's whale, or conquer Mount Sinai with a putter?

Luxury Hearse
An Australian funeral director is offering a highly unusual hearse with its own minibar, DVD player, and fresh coffee-maker. The luxurious mint-green vehicle, which can be hired from Tobin Brothers of Melbourne, is fitted with chrome handrails, tinted windows, pop-out cup holders, and atmospheric lighting. It can hold up to 12 mourners and a coffin.

Novelty Coffins
Coffin-maker Vic Fearn, from Nottingham, England, likes to offer a funeral with a difference. Mr. Fearn makes novelty coffins to cater for every taste and interest, in such diverse shapes as a sports bag, a kite, a canal boat, and a guitar.

> Every year, the **Israeli post office** in **JERUSALEM** sorts up to **3,000** letters addressed to **"God"** and forwards them to the **Western Wall**, where they are inserted into the **cracks** at the **holy site**.

Dolphin Mystery
In August 2003, locals reported a strange sighting on Florida's Gasparilla Lake—a dolphin. Yet the lake is totally landlocked, with no access to the Gulf of Mexico!

Duck March
Guests at the Peabody Hotel, Memphis, Tennessee, witness a truly strange ritual. Twice a day—at 11 a.m. and 5 p.m.—ducks march in a line from their rooftop penthouse to the hotel elevator and then travel down to the marble fountain situated in the hotel lobby. The Peabody Ducks have been a tradition for more than 70 years, dating back to when the hotel manager, Frank Shutt, returned from a drunken hunting trip and thought it would be fun to place some of his living decoy ducks in the hotel's fountain.

▼ Dining on Toilets
A family settle down to a meal in a toilet-themed restaurant named Martun ("toilet" in Chinese), in Kaohsiung, China. Diners sit on toilet seats and the food arrives in bowls shaped like Western-style toilets or Asian-style "squat pots."

Long Payment
At one time, Filipinos could wear their hair long only if they paid a fee of 78 cents a year.

Biggest Cap
Visitors to Rocanville, Saskatchewan, may be amazed to find it is home to an enormous baseball cap. More than 13 times the regular size, it was built from fiberglass in 1988 and sits perched on top of a pole.

Planting the World
For the last five years Ernst and Nelly Hofer have planted a giant maze on their farm. In 2005, they planted a world map. Laid out with GPS, the landmasses are made from feed corn and the oceans are soybeans. One step or stride on the ground in the maze is equal to traveling 43 mi (69 km) on the Earth's surface—that means it would take just 54 strides to cover the breadth of America!

Bathtub Race
The summer of 2005 witnessed the 39th staging of one of Canada's strangest events—the Great International World Championship Bathtub Race, at Nanaimo on Vancouver Island. Motor-powered fiberglass bathtubs—some costing up to $3,000—take to the waters on a 36-mi (58-km) round course. When the race was held back in 1967, the sea was so choppy that only 47 of the 200 starters finished.

Expensive Wind
During the 18th century, in the village of Zaanse in the Netherlands, the government forced windmill owners to pay a tax on the wind.

Free Electricity
John Lorenzen of Woodward, Iowa, who has never paid for electricity, has run his 100-acre (40.5-ha) farm using windmills for over 60 years.

Wheel of Fire
In 1928, a windmill on a farm in Kaltendorf, Germany, began spinning so fast in high winds that it eventually caught fire and burned to the ground.

Reindeer Parking
A hotel in the Siberian city of Nadym announced in March 2005 that it was offering free parking for reindeer! The hotel aimed to cash in on the area's major industry—reindeer breeding.

Park and Pray
Daytona Beach, Florida, boasts its own drive-through church. The congregation park their cars and then listen to sermons delivered from a balcony. During choral songs, some motorists toot their horns instead of clapping.

Inn-credible!
The town of Stafford, in England, lost an entire pub! Workmen dismantled the historic White Lion Inn in 1978 to make way for a new road, but forgot the storage location.

Country for Rent
Located in the Swiss Alps, the entire country of Liechtenstein (with an area of 62 sq mi/160 sq km) can be rented for corporate conferences.

STRANGE WORLD

In-flight Catering
In Canada, a grounded airplane has been turned into a restaurant—Super Connie's Airplane Bar, in Mississauga, Ontario.

Invisible Bar
For years, the town of Nothing lived up to its name. With a population of just four, it was nothing more than a gas station on Hwy 93 between Phoenix and Las Vegas. Then Ben Kenworthy decided to build an invisible bar. Drivers can't see the bar in daylight because the building is camouflaged by thousands of light bulbs, reducing it to a glitter in the Arizona Desert. Passersby can see the light, but assume it is just the sun's reflection.

◄ Hidden Fish
Having flown in from Singapore, a woman was arrested at Melbourne Airport in 2005 after customs officers heard "flipping and flapping noises from the vicinity of her waist." She had 51 live tropical fish in 15 water-filled bags attached to a cutom-made apron hidden under her skirt.

GALLERY
back to the archives

Red Apple House
This apple-shaped store and restaurant stood on a dirt road in Missouri. It had windows all around, a chimney for a stem, and measured 30 ft (9 m) in height and 100 ft (30 m) in circumference.

Herculean Home
Jim Ryan lived in a giant redwood tree called "Hercules," near Dyerville, California. His house had one large circular room that measured 15 ft (4.6 m) in diameter.

Huge Red Piano
The home of the California Piano Supply Co. in Los Angeles was red, shaped like a giant piano, and played piano music on a loudspeaker.

Home on Wheels
John Martie, a sightseer who lost his sight in an accident, built himself a house on his car and covered 50,000 mi (80,465 km) in the U.S.A.

RADIO STORE
Built to resemble an Atwater-Kent radio (c.1935), this storefront in Niles, Michigan, measured 14 ft (4.3 m) high, 9 ft (2.7 m) wide, and 5 ft (1.5 m) deep.

BOTTLE FACTORY
In the 1930s, the Asseline Dairy in Norway, Michigan, was built in the shape of a giant milk bottle. There were three floors of office space for 30 people, connected by a spiral staircase.

CLIMBING HIGH
For 40 years, this magnolia tree in Kent, Ohio, was used to train students of the Davey Tree Expert Co. No man graduated until he could climb the tree without spurs.

PAPER HOUSE
This two-room paper house in Rockport, Massachusetts, has walls and furnishings made entirely from over 100,000 newspapers.

CAR MAIL
An automobile owned by E.G. Hadley from Casper, Wyoming, was covered with 37,770 foreign stamps, from 60 different countries.

Looking Back

October 25, 1799 English captain **Lord Edward Russell** hosted a party where his fountain was used as a punch bowl, into which were added 25 hogsheads (560 gal/2,120 l) of brandy, 25,000 lemons, and 1,300 lb (590 kg) of sugar. **December 28, 1929** When a **boiler** exploded in Canton, Ohio, a man was blown completely through a house 400 yd (366 m) away.

Ripley's Believe It or Not!

Big Boot
A cowboy boot, 39 ft (12 m) tall and weighing 40 tons, looms over Edmonton, Alberta. It was built to promote the Western Boot Factory in 1989, at a cost of $200,000.

Rooftop Goats
A store at Coombs, on Vancouver Island, British Columbia, has goats on the roof! They stay up there during the summer but come down for the winter.

Eye Surgery
Dr. Agarwal's eye hospital in Chennai, Bangalore, India, is shaped like a human eye.

Swimming in Beer
In 2005, an Austrian holiday resort offered guests the chance to swim in a pool of beer. The resort, at Starkenberger in the Tyrol, filled seven pools with around 42,000 pt (20,000 l) of beer, claiming that beer helps to heal a variety of skin diseases.

▶ Monster Machine
A giant sculpture of the Gundam robot cartoon character made from steel and fiberglass appeared in Shiokaze Park in Tokyo, Japan. The structure, which lights up at night, stands 59 ft (18 m) tall and weighs 70,000 lb (31,751 kg), about the same as 30 cars. In just two weeks over 800,000 people had visited the new robot, erected to celebrate the 30-year anniversary of the Gundam cartoons.

Green Monument
In 1971, when war broke out with Pakistan, archeologists in India draped the famous Taj Mahal monument with green cloth to try to camouflage it.

Old Stairs
Archeologists in Hallstatt, Austria, have discovered an ancient wooden staircase, which was preserved in a salt mine, and is more than 3,000 years old.

Scented Food
An Argentinean restaurant has started adding designer perfumes to its dishes. Sifones and Dragones, in Buenos Aires, call their cuisine Pop Food. The menu includes oysters flavored with Anaïs Anaïs, and Chanel No.5 ice cream.

Batman Hotel
At the Hilton, Buenos Aires, Argentina, you can stay in a replica of the Batcave! The room is dedicated to Batman and there is even a secret passage leading from the "cave" to the next room.

To promote its art exhibition **The Naked Truth**, the **LEOPOLD MUSEUM** in Vienna, Austria, announced in 2005 that it was offering **free admission** to anyone who turned up in the **nude!**

IN DEPTH
On The Line

Norwegian slackliner Eiliv Ruud walks across crevasses and canyons thousands of feet above the ground—balancing on a moving rope that is 1 in (2.5 cm) wide.

How did you discover slacklining?

"I'm a professional mountain guide, and climb all over the world. In 1999 in Australia I saw some climbers who had strung a climbing rope between two trees and were balancing on it—a rest day activity. The line, or webbing, is about an inch wide, or less—it's called a slackline because it's not taut. It bounces and sways when you step onto it."

What is a highline?

"It's a slackline that is fixed much higher off the ground. Slacklining was started by American climbers in the late 1980s, although similar acts have been going on in circuses for years. The only difference between walking a low slackline and a highline is a mental one—it's all in your head."

Where did you do your first highline?

"My first one was across a crevasse on a glacier in Chamonix, France. On a high one like that, I have to empty my head of all thoughts—if you're not totally in the moment you will fall off. Highlining is almost like meditation. The lowline is more gymnastic—you can do more because you're not afraid to fall off."

What is the highest line you have ever walked?

"I did the Lost Arrow Spire in California's Yosemite National Park. It was 20 m long and 1,000 m high, and the rigging took us two days to put up. I don't think highlining has been done anywhere higher. I had been training on the same length line lower down and was completely comfortable, but when I first stepped onto it up there my feet just wobbled. I could barely stand, but I kept trying and eventually did it. That was a big one."

How do you train and prepare?

"You can learn the basics of slacklining in a couple of days—after that, it's just practice. The only training for the high ones is mental. You have to be confident in your skills. Before a highline walk I check the rigging, and check it again."

Have you ever lost your concentration or your balance?

"I've started to relax too soon and thought 'Oh I'm almost across now' and then lost it. People do tricks like going backwards, turns, sitting or lying down on their backs, even back flips and handstands, but you still have to really concentrate—if you don't you'll just get halfway across and get thrown off."

What is the worst thing that could happen on a highline?

"If you don't do the rigging properly, the equipment could fail! On a highline, the results could be fatal. If I fall, I usually catch myself with the crook of my knee on the line and hang upside down. You actually get more injuries from the low lines because they bounce and can turn you upside down onto your head."

Is there anywhere you still want to do a highline?

"I would love to do a highline between the spires on the 3500-ft Troll Wall in Norway. But it doesn't matter really where you do it, as long as you are having fun. I've done it over lakes, rivers, glaciers, canyons, and across waterfalls. Being out in the nature surrounded by magnificent scenery is an important part of the experience. But once you're high up on a difficult line you often don't pay much attention to the scenery, because you have to stay so focused on the task at hand."

Eiffel Replica
If you go to Paris, you expect to see the Eiffel Tower, but not one that is only 60 ft (18 m) tall. But that's what you'll find at Paris, Tennessee—a replica of the French original created by Dr. Tom Morrison using 6,000 steel rods and 500 pieces of Douglas fir. The American tower was originally on display at Christian Brothers University in Memphis, but in 1992 it was moved to Paris.

▼ Dish of the Day
Most people cook beneath the hood of an oven, but Bob Blumer prefers cooking beneath the hood of a car. Hollywood's Surreal Gourmet, Blumer has championed cooking meat and fish in aluminum foil on car engines. His recipes often begin: "Preheat the engine for 20 miles...." He has also toured the States promoting his unusual recipes in his "Toastermobile," a trailer equipped with a professional kitchen, and topped with two slices of toast, 8 ft (2.4 m) high!

Cozy Rabbits
William Schultz of Grants Pass, Oregon, heats his greenhouse with the body heat of 350 caged rabbits!

Army Decoy
During World War II, the British magician Jasper Maskelyne was recruited to create an entire fake seaport to hide the Suez Canal and to disguise the activities of the army by building decoy troops. He acheived this amazing deception by using mirrors, flashing lights, and an array of wooden props.

Dead Ends
Alliance, Ohio, is the only town in the whole of the U.S.A. that has a main street that is a dead end at both of its ends.

Paperweight Museum
A museum at Cambridge, Ohio, boasts over 4,000 paperweights. The Degenhart Paperweight Museum houses the collection of former glass-factory owner Elizabeth Degenhart, who picked up her paperweights between 1947 and her death in 1978.

Going Nowhere
Eccentric British tycoon Joseph Williamson dug a network of tunnels under the city of Liverpool, England, 200 years ago. Most of the tunnels lead nowhere.

Banana Stamp
There was once an official stamp issued by the country of Tonga (in the South Pacific) shaped like a banana.

STRANGE WORLD

Mountain Job

In August 2005, executives of ImageNet Co. gave job applicants an initiative test by holding interviews at 12,388 ft (3,776 m) at the summit of Mount Fuji! They wanted to make sure that new employees would have what it takes to scale the heights of business.

Interviewing a prospective candidate on Mount Fuji.

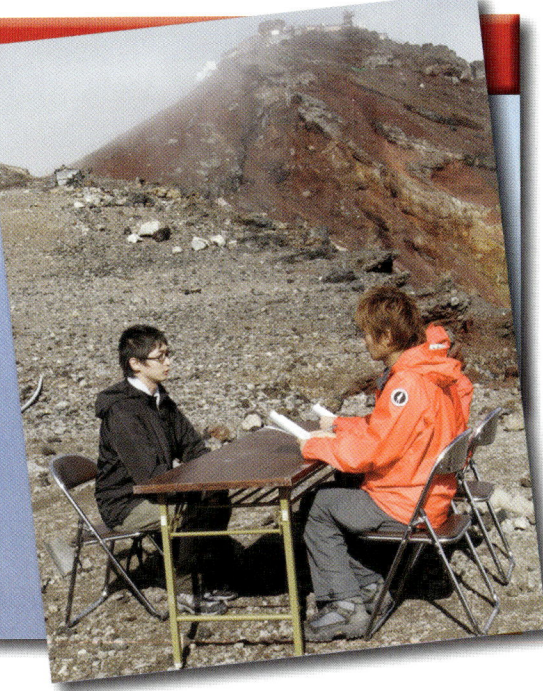

Revolving Jail

At Council Bluffs, Iowa, is a curious three-storey jail known as the Squirrel Cage. Built in 1885, the cells used to revolve constantly so the jailer could watch his prisoners at all times.

Snail Mail

A letter sent to the German town of Ostheim-vor-der-Rhoen in 1718 arrived in 2004, surviving 286 years in the postal system.

The King's Stamp

The king of rock 'n' roll, Elvis Presley, is the only person whose image appears on a U.S. postage stamp approved by a public vote.

Sewer Constrictor

In October 2005, in Manchester, England, a 10-ft (3-m) boa constrictor appeared in an apartment toilet bowl. A concrete block was placed on the toilet lid to prevent the snake escaping before firefighters and plumbers arrived. Using hi-tech fiber-optic equipment, they checked the sewage pipes, but could find no evidence of the snake. Another resident in the apartment building then captured the snake, having found it on his bathroom floor. The snake appeared to have been living happily in the apartments' sewage system!

Tree Hotel

The Hotel Woodpecker, Vasteras, Sweden, sits 43 ft (13 m) above ground in an oak tree in the middle of a park. To reach their rooms, guests must climb a ladder (which is then removed) and meals are served via a basket attached to a pulley.

Luxury Cave

Kokopelli's Cave Bed and Breakfast is surely the world's most luxurious cave. Carved into the side of a mountain in Farmington, New Mexico, the cave covers 1,650 sq ft (153 sq m) and has every modern convenience for guests, including hot and cold running water, carpets, and a kitchen.

Cross Garden

William C. Rice, who died in 2004, erected hundreds of crosses on his land at Prattville, Alabama. It took him more than 20 years to create his garden of faith. Beside the crosses he painted messages of redemption on recycled window air-conditioner covers, refrigerator doors, and auto parts.

State View

On a clear day you can see five states from the top of the Empire State Building in New York City—New York State, New Jersey, Connecticut, Massachusetts, and Pennsylvania.

Dem Bones Dem Bones

A chapel in the Czech Republic contains beautiful decorations and furnishings—and they're all made from human skeletons.

Below is one of the chapel's bone chalices. The use of bones to create this and all the other decorations was intended to give the visitor an impression of the shortness of life and the inevitability of death.

Centuries ago, the abbey at Sedlec was a major burial site. Around 1400, a church was built in the middle of the cemetery and a small chapel was used as an ossuary for the mass graves unearthed during construction.

The task of exhuming skeletons and stacking their bones was given to a half-blind monk.

In 1870, wood-carver Frantisek Rint was employed by the Schwarzenberg family, who owned the church, to put the bone heaps in order. He turned 40,000 skeletons into amazing artistic creations, producing crosses, columns, and chalices of bone. From the center of the nave hangs an enormous chandelier featuring every bone in the human body several times over. Garlands of skulls drape the vaults, four bell-shaped bone mounds occupy the corners of the chapel, monstrances of bones flank the altar, and there is even a bone replica of the Schwarzenberg coat-of-arms.

Above is a detail from a pinnacle: a decorative pyramid of bones. Each pinnacle in the chapel is crowned with a cherub.

STRANGE WORLD

The image on the left shows a cross-shaped decoration above the entrance to the chapel. Below is one of the two solar crosses that are placed in the recesses on either side of the altar.

The bones come mainly from victims of the Black Death plague that swept across Europe in the 14th century, when 30,000 people were buried in Sedlec Cemetery. Some, however, are also casualties from the Hussite Wars of the 15th century—on some of the skulls the marks of battle wounds are clearly visible.

Ripley's Believe It or Not!

Climate Change
Mount Waialeale on the island of Kauai, Hawaii, often has 350 days of rain a year. Yet a few miles away at sea level, the annual rainfall is as low as 20 in (50 cm).

Highs and Lows
Mount Whitney, California, which is the highest peak in the U.S.A. outside Alaska, and Zabriskie Point in Death Valley, which is the lowest point in the U.S.A., are fewer than 80 mi (130 km) apart.

Barrel Boat
Japanese sailor Kenichi Horie, aged 60, spent three months sailing alone across the Pacific Ocean on a yacht made out of beer kegs.

Pepper Shakers
Some people collect stamps, others collect coins, but Andrea Ludden collects salt and pepper shakers. Her 20-year obsession is displayed at the Salt and Pepper Museum in Gatlinburg, Tennessee. And with more than 17,000 shakers from all over the world, her collection is definitely not to be sneezed at!

An **advertisement** in the 1860s for the PONY EXPRESS COMPANY read "must be expert riders, **willing to risk death daily**. ORPHANS preferred."

Tree Huggers
If you thought climbing trees was only for small boys, think again. In August 2005, 52 tree-climbers from across the world scrambled up trunks at a staggering pace for the International Tree Climbing Competition in Nashville, Tennessee. Judging is strict, with penalties for unsafe maneuvers and bonuses for creativity, confidence, and use of equipment. The top prize of $1,000 went to the newly crowned world champions, Dan Krause of Seattle, Washington, and Chrissy Spence from New Zealand.

Windmill King
Frank Medina was acknowledged as king of the windmills. He built up a collection of more than 2,000 windmills at Stockton, in California. At the age of 96, he also had all his own teeth and had never had a cavity!

▶ Ice Sculpture
Randy Finch, from Grand Rapids, Michigan, has built a double Ferris wheel out of ice—that actually works! The sculpture is made from over 30 separate pieces of ice, most less than 1 in (2.5 cm) thick. Each of the individual carts turns on an ice axle. Finch has also made a full-sized ice pool table (above), complete with ice balls and cues.

STRANGE WORLD

Cave Music
The Great Stalacpipe Organ, in the Luray Caverns of Virginia, is a gigantic musical instrument that covers 3.5 acres (1.4 ha). Invented in 1954, the organ uses natural stalactites instead of metal pipes to make beautiful music. Its inventor, mathematician and scientist Leland Sprinkle, walked the length of the caverns, deliberately choosing stalactites that would perfectly match the musical scale.

Colorado Keys
The Baldpate Inn in Estes Park, Colorado, has more than 20,000 keys on display. The collection boasts keys from Mozart's wine cellar, the Pentagon, and Westminster Abbey.

Underground Church
The amazing 750-year-old Church of St. George in the Ethiopian village of Lalibela is built vertically downward! It has been cut out of the rock in the shape of a cross and is surrounded by a trench. The top of the church is flush with ground level. There are 10 other underground churches in the area, many connected by tunnels.

Kicking the Bottle
Bottle Kicking (and Hare Pie Scrambling) competitions have taken place on Easter Monday in Leicestershire, England, since 1771. Yet this curious sport involves neither bottles nor kicking. The contest—often bloody and brutal—takes place between the neighboring villages of Hallaton and Medbourne. The rival villagers fight over three small beer barrels and attempt to manhandle two of them over their opponents' line. The respective goal-lines are two streams a mile apart. The free-for-all has no other rules and the game can last for several hours.

Long Overdue
Padma Maya Gurung, of Nepal, spent an extra six years in jail because a letter of release from the supreme court, issued in 1997, was lost in the mail.

Unexpected Guests
Visitors to a luxury manor house in Kenya are likely to be joined at the dinner table by some unusual guests—a herd of giraffes! Set in 120 acres (49 ha) of forest on the outskirts of Nairobi, Giraffe Manor has welcomed the likes of Mick Jagger, Johnny Carson, Brooke Shields, and Lee Remick. But it is the rare Rothschilds' giraffes that have been the star attractions since moving in to the manor in 1974.

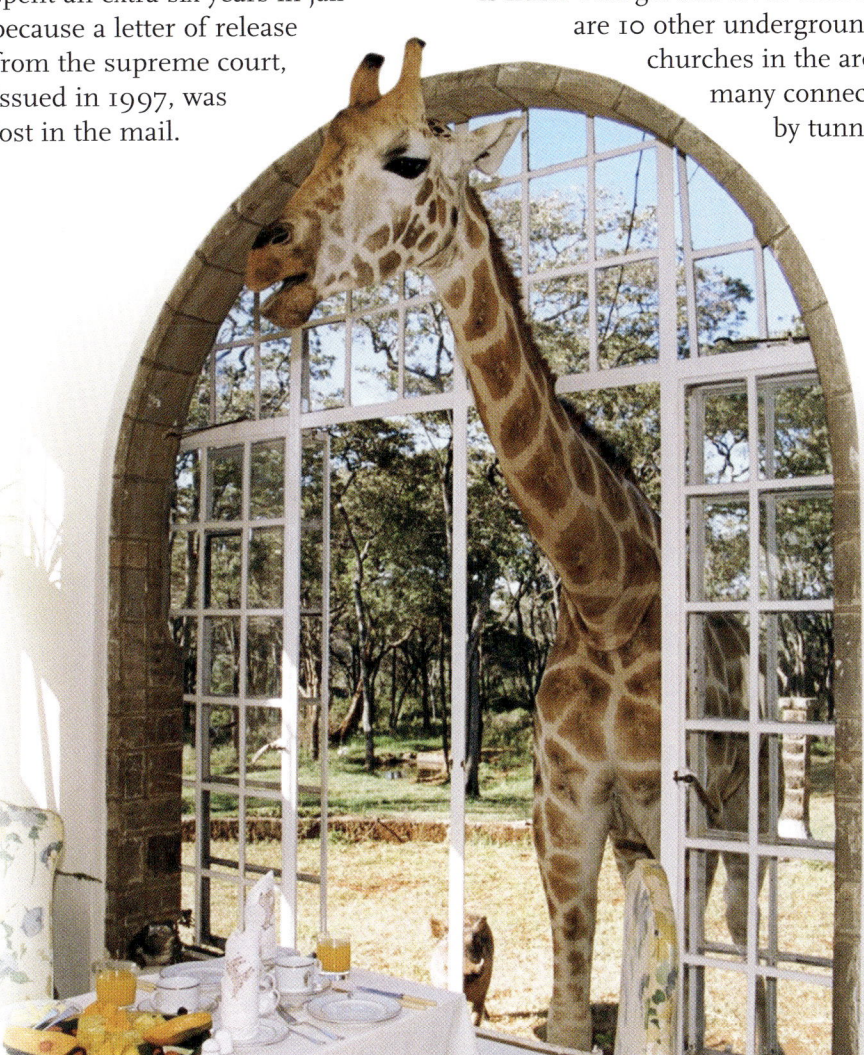

23

MUSEUMS St. Augustine

Ripley's first, oldest, and largest permanent museum, St. Augustine was opened on December 9, 1950. It is situated in a historic 1887 building that was once a hotel where Ripley himself stayed several times in the 1940s. The museum features a full-size Ferris wheel made from Meccano.

SNAKE MASK
This colorful Ceylonese mask, is used to help exorcise evil spirits.

IRON MAIDEN
A medieval German torture device, this was used on heretics to ensure a painful death.

MUMMIFIED CAT
This cat lived over 2,000 years ago in the ancient Egyptian city of Bubastis.

MECCANO TRAIN
Made around 1940, this train is created from hundreds of small pieces of metal "Meccano."

SKULL BOWL
Tibetan monks used to drink blood and wine from this bowl made out of a human skull.

MADE OF MONEY
Macerated money was used to make this sculpture of George Washington.

ROBERT EARL HUGHES
At the age of 20, Robert had a 9 ft 1 in (2.7 m) waist. On his death at the age of 32 he weighed 1,069 lb (485 kg).

WOOD FACE
Using only minimal cuts, this face was created by highlighting lines and patterns already present in the wood.

DON'T MISS!

- Full grown six-legged cow
- Fiji mermaid
- Oriental cabinet from Ripley's house
- Papa Doc Duvalier wax voodoo doll
- Jade ship
- Camel bone carving
- Ripley's personal beer steins
- T-Rex dinosaur skull
- Grandfather clock made from clothes pegs

Ripley's Believe It or Not!

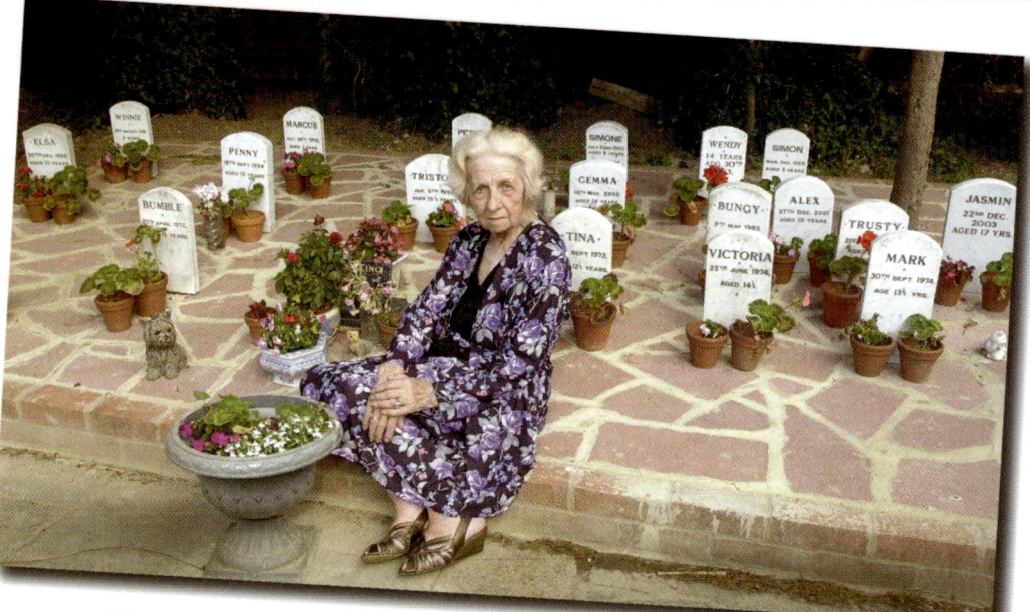

🔺 Pet Cemetery
Jean Pyke has buried 22 pets in her garden on Hayling Island in England. Alongside the pets are also buried the ashes of her dead husband.

House of Clocks
In 1960, Ray Thougen rescued a grandfather clock from a garbage truck and bought three other junk clocks for $5. That was the start of a clock collection that now stands at almost a thousand pieces—all in full working order. For 17 years, Thougen lovingly restored damaged clocks, often without diagrams, before the collection was bought by Ray Sweeney in 1977. Unable to deny the passing of time, both Rays are now dead, but their legacy ticks on at the House of Clocks, in Waukon, Iowa.

Nuts and Bolts
★ The Grand Mosque Djenne in Mali is 328 ft (100 m) long and 131 ft (40 m) wide—and is made from mud!

★ There are over 130 million items on about 530 mi (853 km) of bookshelves in the Library of Congress, Washington D.C.

★ An old-style red telephone kiosk in Huddersfield, England, was converted into a tiny public bar.

Dog Paddle
Among the 500 swimmers that competed in the South End Rowing Club's annual Alcatraz Invitational in 2005, one stood out—Jake the golden retriever. The only four-legged competitor in the field, Jake jumped from a boat near Alcatraz and swam 1.2 mi (1.9 km) to the San Francisco shoreline, finishing a creditable 72nd.

Kahului, *Hawaii*, is home to a museum devoted solely to **paper airplanes**. There are more than **2,000** models ranging from **postage-stamp** size to paper planes with wingspans of **more than 6 ft (1.8 m)**.

Bone Cabin
Near Medicine Bay, Wyoming, is a cabin built entirely from dinosaur bones. Thomas Boylan began collecting discarded bone fragments from a nearby paleontological dig in 1916. Seventeen years later, he had managed to amass an amazing 5,796 bones, weighing a total of 102,116 lb (46,319 kg), which he then decided to use to construct a lodge measuring 29 ft (8.8 m) long and 19 ft (5.8 m) wide.

Duck Walk
Carp collect in such numbers and at such a high density at the base of the spillway of the Pymatuning Reservoir near the town of Linesville, Pennsylvania, that ducks are able to walk across the backs of the fish and hardly get their feet wet!

Symbolic Pot
Towering over the town of Davidson, Saskatchewan, is a coffee pot 24 ft (7.3 m) tall that could hold 150,000 8-oz (227-g) cups of coffee. The giant pot is intended as a symbol of Davidson's friendliness and hospitality.

▶ A Meal Too Far
A Burmese python 13 ft (4 m) long bit off more than it could chew when it tried to swallow whole a 6 ft (1.8 m) American alligator. Both animals were found dead, floating in the water. Experts think the alligator was still alive when the snake swallowed it snout first, and that repeated kicks from its hind legs ruptured the snake's stomach wall.

STRANGE WORLD

Gone to Pot
The site of the Sky Kingdom religious sect in Kampung Batu, Malaysia, was dominated, until its demolition in 2005, by a two-storey building in the shape of a giant pink teapot. The teapot was apparently inspired by the dreams of one of the sect's followers.

Horn Tree
Believe it or not, at Junction, Texas, there is a Christmas tree made entirely from deer horns!

Doll Habit
At Indian River, Michigan, is a museum with around 525 dolls, all dressed as nuns. The Cross in the Woods Nun Doll Museum is the brainchild of Sally Rogalski, who, as a young girl in 1945, used to dress her dolls in nuns' habits to preserve Catholic history. The Rogalskis received a special blessing from Pope John Paul II for their work "in helping to promote vocations to the priesthood and religious life through their doll collection."

Beer-can Castle
Faced with a growing pile of empty beer cans, Vietnam veteran Donald Espinoza from Anonito, Colorado, decided to put them to good use. He spent the following 25 years building a fortress—named Cano's Castle—from the cans, as well as from hubcaps and strips of aluminum.

Ship Shape
A car wash at Eau Claire, Wisconsin, is shaped like a cruise liner, complete with two smoke stacks.

Large wads of alligator skin were found in what remained of the snake's stomach, and the alligator had also sustained wounds behind the eyes and on the shoulder. Until an alligator's spinal cord is severed, it can still move its legs, so its sharp claws could have torn through the snake's skin, causing the gaping hole.

After the snake died, its head was probably eaten by another alligator.

The alligator's tail and hind legs are protruding from a large hole where the python's body literally burst under the pressure of its meal! The stomach of the python still surrounds the head, shoulders, and forelimbs of the alligator.

Moving Land
The fastest-moving place on the Earth is the South Pacific island of Niuatoputapu. It is moving at a rate of 10 in (25 cm) a year.

Fish Parade
The town of Aitkin, Minnesota, hosts an annual Fish House Parade. Fish houses (the sort used for ice fishing) are dressed in weird and wonderful themes and paraded through town for eight blocks before up to 6,000 enthusiastic spectators.

▼ Grape Time
Revellers frolic among grape pulp during the annual grape battle in Binissalem on the Spanish island of Mallorca. The town celebrates its wine tradition with the fiesta every year at the end of the grape festival.

Silent Mourning
Women of the Warramunga tribe of Australia do not speak for a year after the death of their husbands—communicating instead only with hand and arm gestures.

Tiny Congregation
A wooden church in Drumheller, Alberta, is just 11 ft (3.4 m) long and 7 ft (2 m) wide. Originally built in 1968, Little Church has six one-person pews and a pulpit.

Bank Pets
Customers at the Union Federal Savings and Loan Bank in Kewanee, Illinois, can watch two otters, Andy and Oscar, romping in a climate-controlled play pool in the middle of the bank. They were introduced in 1991 by the bank's president.

Firm Bite
Australian Rugby player Shane Millard was treated for an unusual head wound after a match. Doctors found a tooth from one of his opponents embedded in his skull.

Pyramid House
Jim and Linda Onan wanted a house with a difference, so they created a six-story building shaped like a pyramid and made out of 24-carat gold plate. The Gold Pyramid, which is in Wadsworth, Illinois, has an interior that measures an enormous 17,000 sq ft (1,580 sq m). Furnished in the style of the ancient Egyptian pharaohs, it contains a replica of King Tutankhamen's tomb, while the grounds feature a triple-pyramid garage and a 64-ft (19.5-m) statue of the Egyptian king Ramses.

STRANGE WORLD

Wreck Replica
The world's most bizarre Stonehenge replica can be found near Alliance, Nebraska, made entirely from wrecked cars. Built by Jim Reinders in 1987, "Carhenge" has 38 cars, positioned in a circle 96 ft (29 m) in diameter, echoing its famous English counterpart.

Roadside Oddity
In 1930, to catch the eye of passing motorists, brothers Elmer and Henry Nickle built a roadside gas station at Powell, Tennessee—in the shape of an airplane. More recently the airplane building, complete with wings and a propeller, has been used as a car lot.

Junk House
When eccentric sculptor Art Beal bought a hillside plot at Cambria, California, in 1928 he set about building a junk house. He spent 50 years realizing his dream and, as the town's garbage collector in the 1940s and 1950s, he used the junk he collected in the construction. He called the result Nitt Witt Ridge, Beal's alias being Captain Nitt Witt.

Elephant Hotel
In 1881, James T. Lafferty built a hotel in the shape of an elephant. Nicknamed Lucy, this historical landmark is now located in Margate, New Jersey. Lucy is 65 ft (19.8 m) tall and weighs 90 tons. For $4 you can wander through its pink rooms and get an elephant's-eye view of the city.

Easier than ABC
Rotokas, a language of the South Pacific, has an alphabet with only 11 letters, comprising six consonants and five vowels.

Trans-Australian Swim
A group of 60 swimmers swam their way across Australia in a pool attached to the back of a truck traveling at 56 mph (90 km/h).

Petrified Dog
Loggers at Waycross, Georgia, looked inside a hollow tree—and found a mummified dog. It was thought the dog had died after getting stuck in the tree, probably 20 years earlier. The petrified dog is now a local tourist attraction and is displayed inside a cross-section of log.

Deep Sleep
Near Västerås, Sweden, is a hotel where guests sleep in an underwater room. The brainchild of artist Mikael Genberg, the bedroom at the Utter Inn is situated 10 ft (3 m) below the surface of Lake Mälaren, with a window offering a panoramic view of passing marine life.

Fish Hotel
One of Chicago's downtown hotels caters solely for fish. This "fish hotel" is a series of small gardens densely planted with pondweed to satisfy the scaly inhabitants of the Chicago River. Some gardens are floating, others submerged, and all of the "rooms" are fitted with underwater cameras so that humans can catch a glimpse of the action.

In **Cleveland**, Ohio, stands a *gigantic* office **rubber stamp**. Made by artist Claes Oldenburg in 1985, the steel structure is **28 ft (8.5 m) tall** and **48 ft (14.6 m) long**.

Remote Island
The uninhabited Bouvet Island in the South Atlantic is probably the world's most remote island. The nearest land—Queen Maud Land in Antarctica— is 1,050 mi (1,690 km) away, and is also uninhabited.

Turtle Power
At Dunseith, North Dakota, a giant turtle has been welded together from over 2,000 steel wheel rims. The head alone weighs more than a ton.

Big Smoke
This giant cigar, made in Miami, Florida, in 1994, is 6 ft (1.8 m) long, 11 in (28 cm) in diameter, and weighs 55 lb (25 kg)—holding enough tobacco to make 3,000 regular no.1-sized cigars! It took two men two weeks to hand roll.

Look Who's Talking
You never know who's talking to you at Vent Haven, as this museum at Fort Mitchell, Kentucky, is home to over 600 ventriloquists' dummies. It is the legacy of W.S. Berger, who collected ventriloquism memorabilia from the early 20th century up until his death in 1972.

Foam Home
At Centralia, Washington State, is a house covered in Styrofoam®™. The owner, former art teacher Richard Tracy, has been working on the house for more than 20 years.

Giant Chair
A steel chair, 33 ft (10 m) high, stands next to a furniture store in Anniston, Alabama. Built in 1981, the structure can withstand winds of up to 85 mph (137 km/h).

Indoor Beach
With 3,350 sq yd (2,800 sq m) of white sand, the Ocean Dome beach, at Miyazaki, Japan, is one of the world's finest. But what makes it unusual is that it is indoors. The beach features plastic palm trees that sway in an artificial breeze, and 13,500 tons of salt-free "sea." A machine creates surf up to 11 ft (3.4 m) high, and even when the giant roof is open the temperature is a warm 86°F (30°C). There's no danger of sunburn or shark attacks and even the surrounding volcanoes are fake. But perhaps the oddest thing about the dome is that the real beach and sea are only 300 yd (275 m) away!

STRANGE WORLD

Movie Theater
The 2,908-ton Shubert Theater in Minneapolis, Minnesota, was moved in one piece to a new site three blocks away in 1999. The theater was transported on rubber wheels for a short journey that took 12 days.

Prophetic Name
When Nancy Araya opened a new restaurant in Santiago, Chile, in 2005, she decided to call it Car Crash because the area was an accident blackspot. But within a few weeks the restaurant had to close after a passing car crashed through the entrance of the building.

Lobster Derby
In a spoof of the Kentucky Derby, lobster racing takes place every May in Aiken, South Carolina, on a track called Lobster Downs. The track is a series of water-filled tanks where progress can be painfully slow. Indeed some lobsters have been known to die mid-race.

▲ Icy Weather
Gale-force north-easterly winds brought freezing temperatures and freakish weather to Lake Geneva, Switzerland, in January 2005. With 70 mph (120 km/h) winds and temperatures of 10°F (−12°C), waves swept over the lake's banks and droplets of water froze instantly on everything they touched.

Canadian Moulette
A popular pastime in rural areas of North America is cow patty bingo. To play, a field is divided into squares, which are wagered on by contestants. The prize goes to whoever has picked the square on which the cow deposits a pat. In 2003, a Canadian firm introduced a variation on this theme, moulette, using a 50-ft (15-m) long roulette board instead of a field. However, protestors said it was cruel to deprive a cow of dirt and grass on which to answer a call of nature.

Pub Grub
A restaurant in Germany enjoyed a rush of reservations in 2005 after adding maggots to the menu. The Espitas restaurant in Dresden served up such delicacies as maggot ice-cream, fried maggots with cactus and corn, maggot salads, and maggot cocktails. Owner Alexander Wolf said, "We were fully booked for weeks. Most people were disgusted but tried them out of curiosity or for a dare, and were amazed at how good the maggots tasted."

Fence Forte

Musician Simon Dagg from Kent, England, is so obsessed with his first love that he spent a whopping £60,000 ($105,000) fine-tuning the fence around his house so that it would play like a giant glockenspiel. He worked 12 hours a day for five years tuning the metal bars to play like the real thing.

Simon Dagg's musical garden fence measures 120 ft (36.5 m) long.

Tree Village

Believe it or not, the grounds of Alnwick Castle, England, are home to a remarkable tree house—or, rather, a 60-ft (18.3-m) high tree "village"—set among the branches of 16 lime trees. The brainchild of Jane, Duchess of Northumberland, it opened in January 2005, having cost over £3.3 million ($5.7 million). There are five rooms, which include a restaurant, and 6,000 sq ft (557 sq m) of suspended walkways.

Seasonal Snowman

A smiling snowman, 35 ft (10.6 m) tall, stands near Beardmore, Ontario. Made of wood over a steel frame, the snowman was built in 1960 to promote the community and the local ski hill. He even dresses for the time of year—in summer he has sunglasses and a fishing pole; in winter he wears a scarf and carries a curling broom.

On the Border

The Hotel Arbez at Les Rousses straddles the French–Swiss border and offers guests a choice of rooms in either France or Switzerland.

◀ Upside-down Bed

Fancy sleeping in an Upside Down Room, where all the furniture is suspended from the ceiling and you sleep and sit in boxes beneath the floorboards? Or how about the Symbol Room (above), made from 300 square, wooden plates decorated with black-and-white symbols? What about the Coffin Room or the Padded Cell Room? Propeller Island City Lodge Hotel in Berlin, Germany, has 30 rooms, each with a unique, wacky theme.

STRANGE WORLD

► Backwards Biking
Some people aren't satisfied with riding a bicycle the conventional way—they prefer to ride it backwards. In this curious sport, the rider sits on the handlebars instead of the seat, facing backwards, and peddling and steering in reverse! The bikes are not fitted with mirrors or any special adaptations. In 2002, Dutchman and expert backward-cyclist Pieter de Hart cycled an amazing 16.7 mi (26.9 km) in one hour.

Car Spike
The parking lot at the Cermak Plaza Shopping Centre, Berwyn, Illinois, looks like the scene of a horrific accident—shoppers turn a corner to discover eight cars impaled on a 40-ft (12-m) spike! Luckily, it is only a sculpture, named "The Spindle," created by Californian artist Dustin Shuler, from Los Angeles, in 1989.

Monkey Mayor
When the residents of Hartlepool, England, voted for a new mayor in 2002, they elected a man in a monkey costume! H'Angus the Monkey, mascot of the town's soccer team, campaigned successfully with the slogan "free bananas for schoolchildren."

Frog Race
Since 1946, Rayne, Louisiana, has hosted a Frog Derby. Girls from the town dress up frogs in jockey uniforms and encourage them to hop along a course.

Tree Tunnel
You can drive through trees at Leggett, California. The bases of giant redwoods have been tunneled out so that cars can pass through.

TWO HARBORS, Minnesota, must be the only place in the world that has a **museum** devoted solely to **sandpaper**. The collection is located in the house of **John Dwan**, one of the founders of the 3M Company. As a special treat, visitors are given **free** sandpaper samples.

Fireproof City
The Bolivian capital, La Paz, is very nearly fireproof. Located 12,000 ft (3,660 m) above sea level, there is barely enough oxygen in the air to support combustion.

Magnetic Hill
Bizarrely, cars seem to roll uphill at Magnetic Hill, near Moncton, New Brunswick. The phenomenon was first noticed in the 19th century when farmers observed their horses straining to pull wagons down the hill, but when going uphill the wagons would bunch up at the horses' feet. Today, tourists drive their cars to the foot of the hill, stop, put them into neutral and then coast backward, uphill.

The Goat King
For three days a year, Ireland is ruled by a goat! Before the Puck Fair, held in Killorglin, Kerry, every August, chief goat-catcher Frank Joy heads into the hills and captures a wild mountain goat. The goat is duly crowned King Puck and placed on an elevated platform in the center of the town square where, from a height of 50 ft (15 m), he looks down on his subjects for the three-day duration of the fair.

Index

A
airplanes
　airplane-shaped gas station 29
　paper models 26
　as restaurant 13
Alliance, Ohio (U.S.A.), dead-end main street 18
alligator, swallowed by python 26, 26–27
alphabet, short 29
apple-shaped store 14
Araya, Nancy (Chl) 31

B
banana-shaped stamps 18
bank, otters in 28
bars
　invisible 13
　in telephone kiosk 26
Barking Sands Beach (U.S.A.) 8
baseball cap, giant 12
Batcave, replica of 16
bathtub race 12
beach, indoor 30, 30
Beal, Art (U.S.A.) 29
beds, upside-down 32, 32
beer, swimming in 16
beer barrels
　Bottle Kicking competition 23
　yacht made of 22
beer cans, fortress built from 27
Berger, W.S. (U.S.A.) 30
Biblical golf course 11
bicycles, cycling backwards 33, 33
bingo, cow patty 31
bites, human 28
Blumer, Bob (U.S.A.) 18, 18
boa constrictor, in sewage system 19, 19
boats see ships
boiler explosion 15
bones
　decorations made from 20, 20–21
　dinosaur bone cabin 26
boot, giant 16
Bottle Kicking competition 23
bottle-shaped office 15, 15
bowl, made from human skull 25
Boyd, Ben (U.S.A.) 10
Boylan, Thomas (U.S.A.) 26
bread rolls, throwing 8
buildings
　apple-shaped store 14, 14
　bottle-shaped office 15, 15
　cruise liner-shaped car wash 27
　dinosaur bone cabin 26
　eye-shaped hospital 16
　gold-plated pyramid 28
　moving theater 31
　mud mosque 26
　piano-shaped store 14, 14
　radio-shaped store 15, 15
　teapot-shaped building 27
　see also churches; houses

C
cabin, dinosaur bone 26
calf, six-legged 8
cans, fortress built from 27
car wash, cruise liner-shaped 27
cars
　cooking food on engines 18, 18
　covered in stamps 15, 15
　crashing into restaurant 31
　house on back of 14, 14
　magnetic hill 33
　as sculpture 33
　Stonehenge replica 29, 29
cats, mummified 24
cave, hotel in 19
cemeteries see graves
chair, giant 30
chocolate moose 8
Christmas tree, deer horn 27
churches
　drive-through 12
　small 28
　underground 23
cigar, giant 30, 30
climbing trees 15, 15, 22
clock collection 26
coffee pot, giant 26
coffins
　novelty coffins 11
　potential explosion 10
　too small 10
coins, statue of Washington made of 25
cooking on car engines 18, 18
cowboy boot, giant 16
cows
　cow patty bingo 31
　six-legged calf 8
Crazy Horse (U.S.A.) 6, 6–7
crosses, garden of faith 19
cruise liner-shaped car wash 27

D
Dagg, Simon (U.K.) 32, 32
de Hart, Pieter (Net) 33, 33
deer horns, Christmas tree made of 27
Degenhart, Elizabeth (U.S.A.) 18
dinosaur bone cabin 26
dogs
　mummified 29
　swimming race 26
dolls, dressed as nuns 27
dolphin, in landlocked lake 11
drive-through church 12
ducks, marching through hotel 11
Dwan, John (U.S.A.) 33

E
Eiffel Tower, replica of 18
electricity, generation by windmills 12
elephants
　elephant-shaped hotel 29, 29
　two-trunked 9, 9
Empire State Building, views from 19
engines, cooking food on 18, 18
Espinoza, Donald (U.S.A.) 27
explosions, boiler 15
eye-shaped hospital 16

F
faces, carved in log 25
Fearn, Vic (U.K.) 11
fence, as glockenspiel 32, 32
Ferris Wheel, ice sculpture of 22
Finch, Randy (U.S.A.) 22
fire safety, La Paz 33
fish
　overcrowding 26
　smuggling 13, 13
fish house parade 28
fishing, nude 8
food
　cooking on car engines 18, 18
　eating maggots 31
　scented with designer perfumes 16
fortress, built from beer cans 27
frog races 33
funerals
　luxury hearses 11
　novelty coffins 11
　see also graves

G
Garbal, Jaroslaw (Pol) 8
gas station, airplane-shaped 29
Genberg, Mikael (Swe) 30
George IV, King of England 10
giraffes, hotel guests 23, 23
glockenspiel, garden fence as 32, 32
goats
　goat king 33
　on roof 16
God, letters to 11
gold-plated pyramid 28
golf course, Biblical 11
grape battle 28, 28
graves
　grave robbers 10
　pet cemetery 26, 26
　glow-in-the-dark gravestones 10
　wacky gravestones 10, 10
　whiskey bottle-shaped gravestone (U.S.A.) 8
greenhouse, heating with caged rabbits (U.S.A.) 18
Gundam robot 16, 16

H
Hadley, E.G. (U.S.A.) 15, 15
hair, long hair fees 12
Hamilton, Alexander, Duke of (U.K.) 10
hearses, luxury 11
Hemond, Maureen (U.S.A.) 8
highlines, tightrope walking 17
hill, magnetic 33
Hofer, Ernst and Nelly (Can) 12, 12–13
Horie, Kenichi (Jap) 22
hotels
　in a cave 19
　elephant-shaped 29, 29
　in a tree 19
　in two countries 32
　underwater 30
　wacky rooms 32, 32
houses
　on back of a car 14, 14
　built of junk 29
　inside redwood tree 14, 14
　made of newspapers 15, 15
　Styrofoam house 30
　in trees 32
Hughes, Robert Earl (U.S.A.) 25
human body, extremely heavy man 25

I
Ice
　freak weather 31, 31
　Ferris Wheel ice sculpture 22
interviews, on Mount Fuji (Jap) 19, 19
iron maiden (torture device) 24
island, fast-moving 28
Jerusalem, letters to God 11
John Paul II, Pope 27
Joy, Frank (Ire) 33
junk house 29

Index

K
Kenworthy, Ben (U.S.A.) 13
keys, collection of 23
Krause, Dan (U.S.A.) 22
Kuhnert, Dick (U.S.A.) 30

L
La Paz, fire safety 33
Lafferty, James T. (U.S.A.) 29, 29
Lambert, Norman (U.S.A.) 8
lawn mowing ban 8
Lenny the Moose (U.S.A.) 8
letters *see* mail
Library of Congress, statistics 26
Lichtenstein, rental for conferences 12
Lincoln, Abraham (U.S.A.) 10
Liverpool (U.K.), tunnels under 18
lobster races 31
log, face carved in 25
Lorenzen, John (U.S.A.) 12
Ludden, Andrea (U.S.A.) 22

M
maggots, eating in restaurants 31
Magnetic Hill (Can) 33
mail
    lengthy delivery time 19
    lost letter 23
main street, dead end 18
Martie, John (U.S.A.) 14, *14*
mask, snake 24
Maskelyne, Jasper (U.K.) 18
Mayercak, Zdeno (U.S.A.) 8
mayor, in monkey costume 33
maze, giant 12, *12–13*
Meccano train 25
Medina, Frank (U.S.A.) 22
Millard, Shane (Aus) 28
money, statue of Washington made of 25
Monkey, H'Angus the (U.K.) 33
moose, chocolate 8
Morrison, Dr. Tom (U.S.A.) 18
mosque, made from mud 26
Mount Fuji (Jap), interviews on 19, *19*
Mount Whitney, California (U.S.A.) 22
mourning, silent 28
mud
    mud buildings 26
    mud slinging 8
Mullen, William T. (U.S.A.) 8
mummified cat 24, *24*
museums, free nude admissions to 16
musical instruments

garden fence glockenspiel 32, *32*
stalactites 23, *23*

N
newspapers, house made of 15, *15*
Nickle, Elmer and Henry (U.S.A.) 29
Northumberland, Jane, Duchess of (U.K.) 32
Nothing (U.S.A.), invisible bar 13
nudes
    fishing 8
    free admission to museum 16
nuns, dolls dressed as 27

O
Oldenburg, Claes (U.S.A.) 30
Onan, Jim and Linda (U.S.A.) 28
otters, in bank 28

P
Padma Maya Gurung (Nep) 23
paper
    house made of newspapers 15, *15*
    model airplanes 26
paperweight museum 18
peashooting, world championship (U.K.) 8
perfumes, food scented with 16
pet cemetery 26, *26*
Philippines, long hair fee 12
piano-shaped store 14, *14*
Pony Express Company (U.S.A.) 22
Poryong Mud Festival (S. Kor) 8
postage stamps
    banana-shaped 18
    car covered in 15, *15*
    images of live people 19
Presley, Elvis, on postage stamps 19
prisons
    lost letter of release 23
    revolving cells 19
pub, lost 12
punch bowl, giant 15
Pyke, Jean (U.K.) 26, *26*
pyramid, gold-plated 28
python, swallowing alligator 26, *26–27*

R
rabbits, heating greenhouse with 18
radio-shaped store 15, *15*

rain, variations in 22
redwood trees
    driving through 33
    house inside 14, *14*
reindeer, free parking 12
Reinders, Jim (U.S.A.) 29, *29*
restaurants
    airplane as 13
    car crashed into 31
    eating maggots in 31
    throwing bread rolls 8
    toilet-themed 11, *11*
Rice, William C. (U.S.A.) 19
Rint, Frantisek (Cze) 20, *20–21*
Ripley Museum, St. Augustine (U.S.A.) 24, *24–25*
robot, cartoon character 16, *16*
Rogalski, Sally (U.S.A.) 27
roof, goats on 16
rubber stamp, large 30
Russell, Lord Edward (U.K.) 15
Ruud, Eiliv (Nor) 17, *17*
Ryan, Jim (U.S.A.) 14, *14*

S
St. Augustine (U.S.A.), Ripley Museum 24, *24–25*
salt and pepper shaker museum 22
sand
    barking sands 8
    indoor beach 30, *30*
sandpaper museum 33
Schultz, William (U.S.A.) 18
Schwarzenberg family (Cze) 20
sculpture
    chocolate moose 8
    Crazy Horse (U.S.A.) 6, *6–7*
    ice Ferris Wheel 22
    impaled cars as 33
    large rubber stamp 30
    statue of Washington made of money 25
    wacky gravestones 10, *10*
seaport, fake 18
sewage system, snake in 19, *19*
ships
    cruise liner-shaped car wash 27
    yacht made of beer kegs 22
shooting, World Peashooting Championship (U.K.) 8
Shubert Theater, Minneapolis (U.S.A.) 31
Shuler, Dustin (U.S.A.) 33
silent mourning 28
skeletons *see* bones
skull, bowl made from 25

slacklining, tightrope walking 17, *17*
snakes
    in sewage system 19, *19*
    mask 24
    swallowing alligator 26, *26–27*
snowman, giant 32
Spence, Chrissy (U.S.A.) 22
Sprinkle, Leland (U.S.A.) 23
staircase, prehistoric 16
stalactites, as musical instruments 23, *23*
stamps *see* postage stamps
statues *see* sculpture
Stonehenge replica 29, *29*
Styrofoam house 30
Suez Canal, hiding (Egy) 18
Sweeney, Ray (U.S.A.) 26
swimming
    in beer 16
    dog in swimming race 26
    indoor beach 30, *30*
    in pool on back of truck 29

T
Taj Mahal (Ind), camouflage 16
tax, on the wind 12
teapot-shaped building 27
telephone kiosk, bar in 26
theater, moving 31
Thougen, Ray (U.S.A.) 26
tick races 30
tightrope walking, slacklining 17, *17*
Tobin Brothers (Aus) 11
toilets
    snake in 19, *19*
    toilet-themed restaurant 11, *11*
torture, iron maiden 24
Tracy, Richard (U.S.A.) 30
trains, Meccano 25
trees
    Christmas tree made of deer horns 27
    climbing 15, *15*, 22
    driving through 33
    hotel in 19
    house inside 14, *14*
    mummified dog in 29
    village in 32
truck, swimming in pool on back of 29
tunnels
    in redwood trees 33
    under Liverpool 18

U
UFOs 11–14
    "flying saucer," origin of 13
    flying saucer experiment 12

Nazi flying discs 13
photographic evidence 13
sighting over Russia 14
UFO, burns from 13
see also aliens
unexplained phenomena 26–28
  age of the universe 8
  America's first manned space flight 10
  American/Russian meeting in space 10
  Barringer crater, Arizona 8
  black hole formation 8
  comets 9
  craft, missing 27
  crop circles 28
  earth measurements 9
  eclipse and the discovery of America 10
  fish in space, first 9
  Jupiter, gravity on 9
  manned space flight, first 9
  Mercury's year 9
  meteorite crater, largest known 8
  Moon landing, early Chinese 7
  Moon
    birth of the 6
    footprints on the 7
    gravity on the 6
    statistics 6
  neutron stars 9, 10
  Pluto, gravity on 9
  showers, unusual 28
  singing "Happy Birthday" in space 10
  spontaneous human combustion 26
  stigmata 27
  stones, moving 28
  Sun statistics 6
  Sun, burning power of the 6
  universe 6–10

V
ventriloquists' dummies, collection of 30
views, from Empire State Building (U.S.A.) 19

W
waistline, extremely heavy man 25
Washington, George, statue made of money (U.S.A.) 25
weight, extremely heavy man 25
Williamson, Joseph (U.K.) 18
wind, tax on 12
windmills
  collection of 22
  electricity generation 12
  fire 12
  tax on the wind 12
Wolf, Alexander (Ger) 31
World War II, fake seaport 18

Y
yacht, made of beer kegs 22

Z
Zabriskie Point, Death Valley (U.S.A.) 22
Ziolkowski, Korczak (U.S.A.) 6

ACKNOWLEDGMENTS

COVER (b/l) Fredrik Schenholm/Ultimate Freedom Photography, (t/r) the surreal gourmet; 4 Fredrik Schenholm/Ultimate Freedom Photography; 6–7 (dp) DPA/Empics; 7 (t) Sergio Pitamitz/Robert Harding/Rex Features, (b) M. Spencer Green/AP/Press Association Images; 8 Hrywniak Bogdan/Empics; 9 (c) Paul Pikel; 10 (t, c/l & b) Masatochi Okauchi/Rex Features, (c/r) www.fuerrot.at/Rex Features; 11 David Lin/Reuters; 12 Norm Betts/Rex Features; 13 (t) Norm Betts/Rex Features, (b/l) Australian Customs Service/Reuters, (b/r) Rex Features; 16 KPA/Zuma/Rex Features; 17 Fredrik Schenholm/Ultimate Freedom Photography; 18 George Whiteside; 19 (t) Yuriko Nakao/Reuters, (b) Phil Noble/Empics; 20–21 David Giles/Camera Press; 22 www.iceguru.com; 23 (t) Luray Caverns, (b) John Paul Brooke/Rex Features; 26 Solent News/Rex Features; 27 Skip Snow, The United States National Parks Service; 28 Dani Cardona/Reuters; 29 (t) Scott Wishart/Rex Features, (b) Camera Press/ED/JM; 30 (t) Paul Pikel, (b) Pacific Press Service/Rex Features; 31 Action Press/Rex Features; 32 (t) Simon Jones/Rex Features, (b/l & b/r) Lars Stroschen/Rex Features; 33 Sean Dempsey/Empics

All other photos are from Corel, PhotoDisc, Digital Vision and Ripley's Entertainment Inc.